Dedicated to Graham and Samantha,
my sources of inspiration.

DREAM,
my child

Andrews McMeel Publishing
a division of Andrews McMeel Universal
1130 Walnut Street, Kansas City, Missouri 64106

www.andrewsmcmeel.com

22 23 24 25 26 SDB 10 9 8 7 6 5 4 3 2 1

ISBN: 978-1-5248-6786-7

Library of Congress Control Number: 2021952349

Editor: Patty Rice
Art Director/Designer: Julie Phillips
Production Editor: Elizabeth A. Garcia
Production Manager: Cliff Koehler

Illustrations: Janie Secker/Lilla Rogers Studio

ATTENTION: SCHOOLS AND BUSINESSES
Andrews McMeel books are available at quantity discounts with bulk
purchase for educational, business, or sales promotional use.
For information, please e-mail the Andrews McMeel Publishing
Special Sales Department:
specialsales@amuniversal.com.

DREAM, my child,

r.h. Sin

Illustrated by Janie Secker

Dream, my child
You'll sleep tonight

Dream, my love

Til morning light

Close your eyes
Beneath the moon

Close your eyes
Til morning blue

Dream, my child
Of stars so bright

Dream, my love
All through the night

Close your eyes
And drift away

Close your eyes
And soon you'll wake

Dream, my child
I'll see you soon

Good night, stars

Good night, moon

Dream of things
That bring you peace

Dream of love
Soon as you sleep

Dream, my child

And have no fear

When you awake

I'll be
right here